New Brunswic.
thru 4/03

DATE DUE   OCT 0 2

FEB 1 3 '03			
MAY 15 '03			
JUL 1 0 '03			
NOV 28 '03			
APR 15 04			
JAN 07 05			
SEP 27 06			
GAYLORD			PRINTED IN U.S.A.

JESSIE HAAS

Chipmunk!

pictures by

JOS. A. SMITH

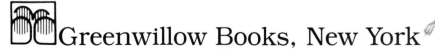

Greenwillow Books, New York

Library of Congress Cataloging-in-Publication Data
Haas, Jessie. Chipmunk! / by Jessie Haas ;
pictures by Jos. A. Smith. p. cm.
   Summary: The bumbling antics of her human owners
cause Puss to lose her captured chipmunk.
   ISBN 0-688-11874-7 (trade). ISBN 0-688-11875-5 (lib. bdg.)
   [1. Chipmunks—Fiction. 2. Cats—Fiction.]
I. Smith, Joseph A. (Joseph Anthony) (date), ill. II. Title.
PZ7.H1129Ch 1993 [E]—dc20 92-30080 CIP AC

For Susan, who is glad I've gone funny
   —J. H.

For Kari, Emily, and Joe, and every child
who dreams of making her or his own run
for the freedom of a tree
   —J. A. S.

All Puss wanted was a place to put her chipmunk so it couldn't get away!

When she grabbed it, the chipmunk wiggled and squeaked.

Puss ran as fast as she could, back to the house and—CLACK!—through the cat-door.

Now Puss could let go. She knew she could find the chipmunk again, as soon as she caught her breath.

All the chipmunk wanted was a place to hide!
ZIP! – it dove into the knitting basket. The basket
tipped. Out tumbled the balls of yarn, and away
they rolled into all the corners.
One ball of yarn had stripes, and tiny little legs....

All the family wanted was to get the chipmunk out!
"Oh no!" cried Mother. "My jade plant!"
"Don't, Puss!" hollered Dad. He grabbed the lamp,
just in time.

Through Ryan's block castle the chipmunk ran.
After it went Puss, and CRASH! went the castle.
"*Puss!*" yelled Ryan. "It wasn't even *finished*!"

"Open the door!" shouted Dad. He grabbed the broom and tried to sweep the chipmunk out. "Oops! Where'd it go?"

"In the cupboard!" Mother cried. "Behind the jars!" Dad reached in with the broom handle and poked out all the jars. Over they fell—CLUNK!—and out spilled the rice, out spilled the sugar—

"There!" said Ryan. "Under the chair!"

All Puss wanted was her chipmunk back.

She pounced.

BANG! – the chair tipped over.

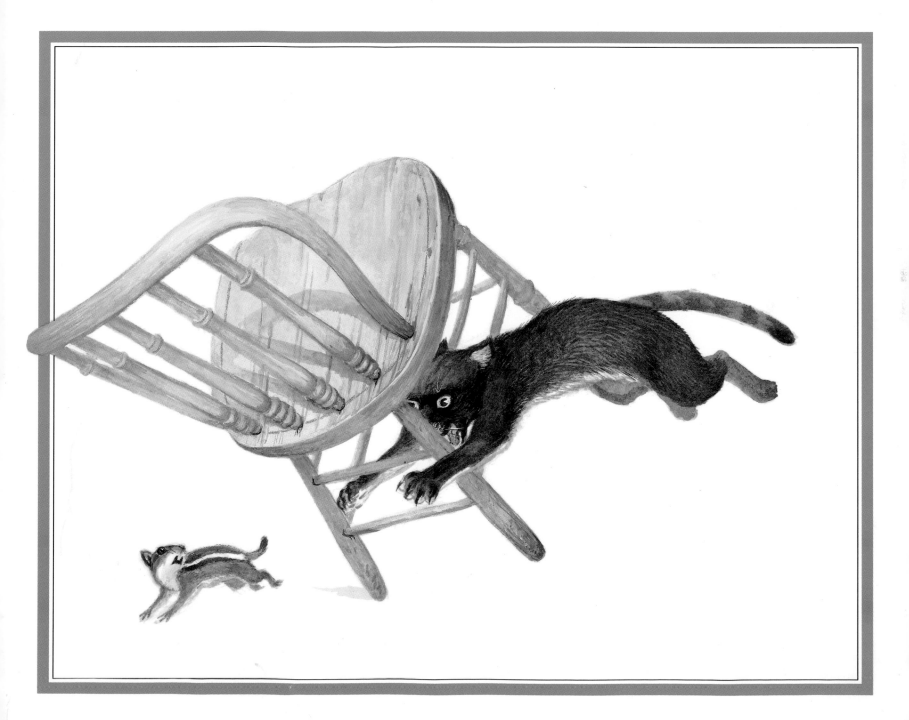

Up Dad's leg the chipmunk ran, and across his shirtfront, and – ZIP! – onto his head.

"Aaaah!" said Dad. He stood very still. "All I want is to get it off me!"

"A towel!" said Mother. "I'll catch it in a towel!"

Puss stood on her hind legs. She sank her claws into Dad's pants. Puss was going to climb up Dad.

"No!" said Ryan. He grabbed Puss. "All it wants is to get out! Walk outside, Dad! Just walk outside!"

"Oh," said Dad. Very carefully, he walked outside. Mother and Ryan and Puss watched through the window.

Dad stood beside a tree.

ZIP! — the chipmunk ran up the trunk.

In a second it was gone.

"Phew!" said Mother. "All I want now is to
clean this house!"
Dad raked all ten fingers through his hair.
"All *I* want is to scratch!"
Ryan sat down in the middle of the blocks.
He rolled one for Puss.
But Puss wouldn't play with it. CLACK!—
she went back out through her catdoor.

All Puss wanted was to catch another chipmunk!